A FRIBBLE MOUSE LI

The Secret of the Silver Key

Phyllis J. Perry

Illustrations by Ron Lipking

W9-AKT-890

Fort Atkinson, Wisconsin

**For Casey, Clare, Julia, and Emily, and for Kenny,
who has learned to dive into reading.**

Published by UpstartBooks
W5527 Highway 106
P.O. Box 800
Fort Atkinson, Wisconsin 53538-0800
1-800-448-4887

Copyright © 2003 by Phyllis J. Perry

The paper used in this publication meets the minimum requirements of American
National Standard for Information Science — Permanence of Paper for Printed
Library Material. ANSI/NISO Z39.48.

Fribble Mouse stood in his front yard playing catch with his little brother, Scamper. Fribble felt proud using two of his brand-new birthday presents; a baseball mitt that smelled of fresh leather, and a shiny white ball with red stitching that didn't have any grass stains on it yet. Instead of dropping almost every ball as he usually did, Scamper was making good catches using Fribble's old glove.

That was a good thing, because Fribble felt too stuffed to bend over, and he surely didn't want to have to chase any balls. In fact, he didn't think he could run anywhere at the moment. Six school friends and his neighbor from across the street, Mr. Crumb, had come to his Saturday afternoon birthday party. Fribble's mother fixed his favorite food, gooey macaroni with tons of cheese.

Afterwards Fribble ate a huge helping of cheesecake. His friends, laughing and full, had left about half an hour ago.

Fribble watched as the red-white-and-blue mail truck made its way slowly down the street. When the mailman reached their house, he put several envelopes in the mailbox and waved at the two ballplayers.

Fribble stopped playing catch and ran to pick up the mail and bring it inside. Without looking at it, Fribble handed over three envelopes and a catalog to his mother, who was in the kitchen, and then headed for the yard again.

"Just a minute, Fribble," his mother said as she turned over the envelopes in her paws, "this one's for you."

"For me?" Fribble's long tail switched back and forth and his whiskers began to quiver as they always did when his curiosity was aroused. Was someone sending him a birthday card? Who could it be?

Mother handed Fribble the envelope and he stared at it. It was addressed to Fribble Mouse all right. No mistake. Then he squeezed it. The envelope had a big, hard lump in it. What was that? Could it be a birthday present?

"Whatcha doing, Fribble?" Scamper called from the doorway.

"I got a letter!" Fribble said.

"Is there one for me?" Scamper asked.

"No, but it's not *your* birthday, is it?" Fribble pointed out. Scamper stood close by to watch.

Fribble tore open the envelope. Inside was a bright birthday card showing a picture of a young mouse in a baseball uniform. Fribble read the front of the card, "Happy Birthday," aloud. Then he opened the card and found a key on a chain tucked inside.

The key was silver, but it wasn't shiny. In fact, it looked old. It was small with a hole through the shaft and a jagged little piece that hung down at the tip.

"What is it?" Scamper asked.

"It's a key," Fribble said.

"I mean, what's it for?" asked Scamper.

"I don't know yet," Fribble said. He carefully put the chain around his neck and then opened the card. A message was written inside. Luckily Grandma had printed it because Fribble didn't know how to read cursive writing yet.

"What's it say?" Scamper asked.

Slowly, because he wasn't the world's best reader, Fribble read out loud, "Dear Fribble, I hope you have a happy birthday with your friends today. Grandpa and I will have another birthday party for you next weekend when you come to visit us on the farm. And we have a special present for you, too. I won't tell you what it is, because that's a secret. But I will tell you that you'll need your key. The key opens your present and it's an antique." Fribble read this last word as "an-tee-cue."

"Aunty Q? Who's that?" Scamper demanded. "I know Aunty Bessie and Aunty Pokey, but I don't know any Aunty Q."

Fribble looked at his mother. She was smiling, but she didn't say anything. Of course Fribble could have *asked* her about the strange word, but he liked to figure things out on his own. He pushed the envelope into his pocket and said to Scamper, "Want to take a walk with me to the library?"

"Sure," Scamper agreed. Cheddarville's library was only a couple of blocks away, and Scamper often went there with Fribble. The librarian, Miss Scurry, was glad to see them because they always had interesting questions for her.

"Hello," she said, as Fribble and Scamper came in. "May I help you with anything today?"

"No, thanks," Fribble said. "I just want to use your dictionary, and I know where you keep it," he added.

Fribble and Scamper went straight to the reference shelf and took the dictionary with them to a big, empty library table. Fribble knew how to use the guide words at the top of the pages, and he knew that a word, like antique, starting with an "a" would be near the front of the dictionary. He pulled the birthday card out of his pocket so he could compare the spelling. It didn't take him long to find "an-ti-que."

Slowly Fribble read the definition aloud to Scamper, "Aunty Q," he said. "It means an object made at an earlier time."

Scamper frowned, and in his excitement, he spoke a lot louder than he meant to. "Does that mean we have a really old aunt?" he asked.

Miss Scurry couldn't help but hear, and she hurried over. "Having a problem?" she asked.

Fribble pointed to the word in the dictionary. "I can't figure this out," he admitted. "Aunty Q means old, but you see, we don't have an Aunty Q at all, young or old."

It was Miss Scurry's turn to be confused. "Aunty Q?" she said. She looked at where Fribble was pointing in the dictionary and smiled. Then she said, "You've found the right word, all right. But you're not pronouncing it correctly. Instead of saying 'Aunty Q,' you say 'an-teek.' And you're absolutely right. An antique is something old. It could be a piece of furniture or a piece of jewelry or even an old spoon," she explained.

"If you look at the word," Miss Scurry continued, "you can see some markings. And those markings tell you how you should say the word out loud."

"I wondered what all those funny marks were," said Fribble. "How can you remember them all?"

"See down here?" asked Miss Scurry, pointing to the bottom of the page. "They give you examples. Sometimes they give the examples in the front of the book."

"I see," Fribble said.

"Now why are you interested in antiques?" she asked. "I thought you were interested in radios and insects and crabs."

Fribble showed Miss Scurry his birthday card, and then he held up the little silver key that he was wearing on a chain around his neck.

"Oooh," she said. "I wonder what antique that key unlocks?"

"So do I," Fribble said.

"Maybe it fits an old pirate's treasure chest," suggested Scamper.

"It's a pretty small key for a pirate's chest," Fribble said. "And I don't think many pirates buried treasure on Grandma and Grandpa's farm." Fribble closed the dictionary and put it back on the reference shelf. He thanked Miss Scurry for her help, and then he and Scamper went home.

Fribble was unusually quiet as they walked, and he smoothed his whiskers. He was busy thinking. What would that key unlock?

As soon as they walked back into the kitchen when they reached home, Fribble's mother asked, "What did you find out at the library?"

"We learned that an 'an-teek' is something real old," Fribble said, stressing the end of the word when he spoke.

"But I still don't know who Aunty Q is," Scamper admitted, shaking his head. He furrowed his brow and stroked his whiskers, copying his brother.

Fribble looked at his little brother and sighed. Once Scamper got the wrong idea in his head, it was very hard to get it out again.

Suddenly, Fribble turned to his mother and asked, "Are antiques valuable?" That question had just occurred to him. His mother and father had given him a new baseball glove for his birthday, and Scamper had given him a brand-new ball. Why would Grandma and Grandpa give him something old and used unless somehow an antique was worth a lot?

"Some of them are," his mother said. "Just a block over on Edam Street, old Miss Slippers runs an antique shop out of her little white cottage. She lives upstairs, but in the downstairs rooms, she keeps lots of beautiful old things for sale. Some of them are very expensive."

"Really?" Fribble asked. He clutched the key hanging around his neck. His tail swished and his whiskers quivered. Next weekend he would become the owner of a valuable antique!

"Is that where Aunty Q lives?" asked Scamper.

Fribble ignored his brother and instead continued questioning his mother. "You mean just a block away, there's an antique shop?"

"Yes," his mother said. "I'm sure you've seen it. There's a big sign out front that says 'antiques.'"

Fribble thought for a moment. "Is it the one where there's an old stove on the front lawn with pots of petunias sitting on top of it?"

"That's the one," his mother said.

"Yeah, I've seen it," Fribble said. "I always thought it was kind of crazy to keep a stove out in the yard. I didn't know it was an antique shop. Can I go there and look around?"

"Me, too?" squeaked Scamper.

"Not by yourselves," his mother said.

"But I know where it is," Fribble insisted. "And I'll hold Scamper's paw when we cross the street. Promise."

"No. If you go inside an antique shop, I have to go with you. I know you'll try to behave yourselves, but many of the valuable antiques are very breakable."

Fribble recognized the firm tone of his mother's voice, and he realized that no amount of pleading would change her mind. "Would *you* take us then?" Fribble asked.

"Certainly not today," Fribble's mother said. "It's late and soon I've got to fix dinner. It's a special one tonight because of your birthday," she added with a smile.

"What about tomorrow?" asked Fribble. Not even tempting food could distract Fribble from his eagerness to visit the antique shop. He loved secrets and mysteries, and he had to find out what sort of surprise his birthday key would open.

"I'm not sure if the antique shop is open on Sundays," his mother said.

"We could walk over and find out," suggested Scamper who was never short of energy. "We wouldn't go in the shop without you, of course," he said to his mother, firmly shaking his head back and forth. "But we could look for a sign that Fribble could read telling us if it's open and watch and see if any customers are going in or out."

"Good thinking," Fribble said. "But I've got a better idea. Since it's a store, the owner probably lists her address and the store hours in an ad in the phone book. Let's look."

Fribble's mother got the big phone book from the shelf and placed it on the table. "Do you remember how to use this?" she asked.

Fribble nodded. "There's all sorts of good information in the front of the book. And then everyone's phone numbers are listed in the white pages," he said. "And last of all, the yellow pages have listings and ads for businesses like antique shops."

"That's right," said Fribble's mother.

Proud that he remembered how to use the telephone book, Fribble opened it to the beginning of the yellow pages. "Antiques will be near the front," he said to his brother confidently, "because everything is listed in alphabetical order, and 'A' for antiques is the first letter of the alphabet."

"I know part of the alphabet," Scamper said proudly. "A, B, C, D, E, F, G, H, I, J, K ..." he hesitated. Then he sighed. "But not all of it, yet."

While Scamper was reciting the alphabet, Fribble was carefully flipping through the pages of the telephone book and reading aloud, stumbling a little over the harder words, "Accountants, air conditioning, ambulance service, antiques."

At this point, Fribble's whiskers began to twitch. He knew he was getting close. "Here it is," he said with a squeak of triumph. He pointed with his paw at each word as he read: "Miss Slippers's Antique Shop. Bringing you the best. Buy, sell, trade, 137 Edam Street, Cheddarville. Mondays through Fridays, 9 a.m. to 5 p.m., Saturdays and Sundays, noon to 5 p.m."

"The store is open on Sunday," Fribble announced excitedly. "Can we go after lunch tomorrow? Please?"

"Well, you'd both have to be on your very best behavior," his mother said. "Because you have to be careful and quiet inside an antique shop. It's not like a toy store where you can handle the cars and trucks, and try zipping them around on the counter, or like a library where you can pick up any book you want. In an antique shop, you *look* at things, but you *don't touch.*"

"We could remember that, couldn't we, Scamper?" Fribble asked solemnly.

Scamper looked very serious as he nodded his head up and down.

"I remember Miss Slippers has a sign just inside the door," Fribble's mother continued. "It's a little poem, and it goes like this: 'Lovely to look at, delightful to hold, but if you break it, consider it sold.'"

"What's that mean?" Scamper asked.

Fribble said, "I think it means if you drop something in her store and break it, you have to pay for it."

"Oh," Scamper said. "I wouldn't want to buy something that was broken."

"Neither would anyone else," his mother explained. "That's the point. But as long as you understand that you can't run around and grab things, I'll take you after lunch tomorrow."

"Thanks," Fribble said.

"Now, why don't you set the table for me and then run along and play while I finish getting our dinner ready?"

Without a murmur, Fribble started setting place mats and plates on the table while Scamper counted out the silverware.

When the table was set, Fribble and Scamper went out and started playing catch again.

As he automatically caught and tossed the ball, being careful not to throw it too hard, Fribble's mind raced. An antique shop, he thought. I'm going to go to an antique shop tomorrow. I'll be sure to take my birthday key. Maybe Miss Slippers will know what sort of thing it opens.

After lunch on Sunday, Fribble and Scamper didn't have to be asked to help clear the table and carry dishes to the kitchen. They were model boys on their very best behavior.

It was a sunny October day, but a little nippy out. Fribble's mother insisted that they wear their jackets, and they didn't argue. Briskly they walked to the corner, crossed the street after Fribble made a great show of looking both ways, and then walked just one block to Edam Street.

Turning left, they looked for number 137. Fribble immediately recognized the white cottage with the stove in the yard and the sign saying "Antiques" hanging over the door. They turned up the walk, and Fribble's mother rang the bell.

Fribble noticed that this was an old-fashioned bell. To operate it, you didn't push a button, but gave a sharp twist, and then a loud "Brrrrrring" sounded inside the house. After just a moment, Miss Slippers appeared.

"Please come in," she said, stepping back to allow Fribble, his mother, and Scamper to enter. "Welcome. Would you like to browse around, or could I help you find something in particular?"

Fribble stared up at Miss Slippers. She looked exactly the way Fribble thought she would. She was an old, white mouse wearing a gray dress with pink roses on it. She was also wearing slippers. Not just any slippers, mind you. These were pale pink with roses that matched her dress. She had kindly eyes and didn't look at all worried that two young boys had entered her shop.

Before anyone else could speak, Scamper asked, "Are you Aunty Q?"

"No, dear," Miss Slippers said, looking puzzled. "My name is Miss Abigail Slippers." Seeing how disappointed he looked, she quickly added, "But you may call me Aunty Q if you like."

Before Scamper could speak again, Fribble pulled the chain holding his birthday key over his head and held it up to Miss Slippers. "Grandma and Grandpa sent me this for my birthday," he blurted out. "Can you tell me what it will open?"

Miss Slippers took the key and said, "Let me take a closer look." Dangling around her neck on a black velvet band were a pair of gold-rimmed reading glasses. She took these and perched them on her nose. "Hmmm," she said, as she turned the key over in her paw and examined it closely.

"I can tell you that you don't use this kind of key to wind a clock or lock a door. My guess is that it opens a desk or a chest of some sort."

"A chest!" Scamper shouted. "I *told* you, Fribble, it's the key to a pirate's chest!"

"Scamper," his mother said, "do I need to remind you to use your indoor voice?"

"Sorry," Scamper said quickly. He lowered his voice, but he went right on talking. "But Aunty Q, I *just knew* it was the key to a pirate's treasure," he insisted.

"I suppose you could be right," Miss Slippers agreed. There was a twinkle in her eye. "You know, in all my years I've never seen a real pirate's chest. But I have seen several desks and chests that this kind of key opens." She walked over to a desk, pulled open one of its drawers, and removed a key tied to a blue ribbon. "See how this works," she said.

Fribble and Scamper crowded near. Miss Slippers put the key that hung from the ribbon into a small hole outlined in brass. Fribble heard the sound of a latch, and then the front section of the desk swung down to make a writing surface.

"The same key works on the drawers underneath, too," Miss Slippers explained. Closing up the writing section again, she showed how the key opened and locked the desk drawers.

Taking the key on the blue ribbon with her, she walked over to a grandfather clock. She took the clock key and showed it to Fribble and Scamper. "See how the key that's used for winding the clock looks different from this desk key?"

"Yeah," Fribble said. "The clock key doesn't have one of those ridges hanging down at the tip."

"That's right," Miss Slippers said. "Your key looks much more like this desk key than the clock key, doesn't it?" Carefully, she handed the birthday key back to Fribble and he slipped the chain over his head. Then she went over to help Fribble's mother, who was admiring cups and saucers.

"I love this tea set," Fribble's mother said. Fribble and Scamper went to see. She held up a cup with a gold lip and handle. Tiny violets were painted inside the cup and around the edge of the saucer.

While his mother and Miss Slippers looked at fancy dishes, Scamper and Fribble wandered around the rest of the store. The front two rooms looked just like a parlor and dining room of a fancy house. There were straight-backed and cushioned chairs, tiny tables with delicate bits of cloth on them, lamps, dishes and vases, clocks, desks, and tables.

Keeping Scamper with him, Fribble made his way to the back rooms. Here things were crowded closer together. On one table, there was jewelry.

"Dad would love this gold watch," Fribble told Scamper, pausing to look at it.

Quietly Miss Slippers came up behind them. "You've found one of my treasures," she said. She picked it up, pressed a button on the side, and opened up the pocket watch to show them the face. "That watch belonged to a Colonel Beauregard Chapman. It's over one hundred years old."

"Oooh," Scamper said. "Does it still work?"

"Yes," Miss Slippers said. "It keeps perfect time. Listen." In turn she held it to each of their ears and let them hear it tick away.

Fribble wandered into another small room. It was filled with toys and games of all sorts. There were old dolls, a child-sized rocking chair, and a hobby horse.

"Aunty Q, could I sit in the chair?" Scamper asked.

"Of course," said Miss Slippers.

As Scamper rocked gently in the tiny chair, Fribble spied something across the room. It was a baseball, balanced on a black marble stand. Fribble scurried over to it. He looked at the ball, stared, blinked, and stared again. No doubt about it. The ball had two names written on it in ink, and one signature was that of his hero, Slugger McGraw. Fribble drew in his breath and whirled around to face Miss Slippers.

"Did Slugger McGraw really sign this ball?" he asked.

"Yes, he did," Miss Slippers said. "Are you a baseball fan?"

"I sure am," Fribble said.

"He plays ball all the time," Scamper chimed in from his cozy chair.

"Well, that's the ball that Slugger McGraw hit for a home run that won the World Series game for the White Paws in 1951," she said.

"Really?" said Fribble. He felt his heart beating fast. "The game that was tied in the ninth inning with two outs, when Slugger came up to bat?"

"That's the one," Miss Slippers said.

"But there are two names on the ball," Fribble said. Slowly he sounded out the second name. "It says Flash Rodgers, doesn't it?"

Miss Slippers put her reading glasses back on her nose. "Yes," she said. Then she frowned. "I don't know who Flash Rodgers is, do you?"

"No," said Fribble. "I never heard of him." He looked at the ball again longingly.

"But I wish I owned that ball. The one that Slugger hit."

"It's rather expensive, I'm afraid," Miss Slippers said. "Two hundred dollars. But keep looking, maybe you'll find something else that you like."

When they finally left the store, Fribble's mother carried a thin crystal vase home with her. "It will be perfect for my roses," she said. And Scamper and

Fribble each left with a piece of wrapped candy from a big bowl on Miss Slippers's desk.

Fribble also took away with him a dream, a dream of owning the baseball that Slugger McGraw hit for a home run. And he had two new questions. Did the key that Grandma sent open a special desk or chest? And who was Flash Rodgers?

As soon as they were home again, Fribble announced that he was going to the library. Of course, Scamper wanted to go, too.

As they came in the door, Miss Scurry greeted them with a smile. "Here to learn more about antiques?" she asked.

"No," said Fribble. "Today we need to use an encyclopedia."

"What are you looking for?" Miss Scurry asked.

"I want to know who Flash Rodgers was," said Fribble.

"I don't recognize that name," Miss Scurry admitted. "Do you know anything about Flash Rodgers?"

"I think he was a baseball player," Fribble said. "His name is on a baseball that Slugger McGraw hit for a home run in the World Series in 1951."

"Aha!" Miss Scurry said. "He probably isn't in the general encyclopedia, but we have some special encyclopedias. There's an encyclopedia of music, an encyclopedia of medicine, and an encyclopedia of sports."

"It's the encyclopedia of sports for us then," Fribble said.

Miss Scurry brought over the encyclopedia of sports and helped them find the section on baseball and information about the 1951 World Series.

Fribble read aloud to Scamper, sounding out the hard words. Finally he saw Flash Rodgers's name. "He was a fast base runner, and he was sent in during the ninth inning to run for Blimpy Monroe. Flash Rodgers scored when he came home on Slugger McGraw's home run," Fribble explained.

Fribble beamed. He had the answer to one of his questions. Now he couldn't wait to answer the other one. What did his birthday key open?

Early Saturday morning, fully dressed and ready to go to Grandma and Grandpa's farm in Muenster, Fribble bounced around the kitchen, far too excited to sit down for breakfast.

"You must eat something," Fribble's mother insisted. She shooed him into a chair and put a plate in front of him. "It's a long drive to the farm. We won't get there until lunchtime. You'll be hungry and cranky all the way unless you have breakfast."

Fribble forced himself to eat a piece of toast, and he had to admit that covered in raspberry jam, it was really very tasty.

Scamper sat across from Fribble. Although Scamper seemed excited too, Fribble noticed that Scamper had no problem tucking away a big meal. Nothing ever seemed to shrink Scamper's appetite. How could anyone so small eat so much?

Everything and everyone was finally packed into the car when Fribble suddenly shouted, "Wait! I forgot my new baseball and glove. I want to bring them so I can play catch with Grandpa."

He leaped out of his seat and ran toward the house.

"Bring the old glove, too," Scamper shouted after him.

Fribble scurried back in and out of the house. He stashed the ball and both gloves on the floor of the back seat, and finally the car drove away. The streets of Cheddarville were soon left behind as they made their way toward the little village of Muenster. The countryside was alive with brilliant colors. Reds and golds splashed all the leaves, marking a spectacular end of summer.

Normally Fribble felt antsy whenever he made a long car trip. But today, he was quiet. Again and again, he fingered the key hanging from his neck. His mind raced over dozens of possibilities as to what the key would open.

They turned off the main road and headed down a dirt lane toward a neat farmhouse with a huge weathered barn behind it. Fribble broke the stillness with a loud shout, "We're here! We're here!"

The car doors flung open, and everyone spilled out at once into the arms of Grandma and Grandpa. After many hugs and greetings, the little group moved inside. Fribble thought the dining table looked splendid with its centerpiece of small pumpkins, dried corn, and a mass of colorful leaves.

Fribble's glance darted from tables and chairs to corners of the room. His long tail lashed through the air, and his whiskers quivered. Where was his birthday present? He knew it wouldn't be polite to ask, but Fribble was about to burst with curiosity. Was it small? Was it large?

Grandma glanced at the clock on the mantle and announced, "Dinner will be served in an hour. That will give Fribble time to open his birthday present before we eat. I see you're wearing your key," she added, turning to smile at him.

Fribble knew he could count on Grandma. Some would have drawn the wait out, but she seemed to understand how excited Fribble was.

"I've got it," Fribble squeaked. He took off the chain with the little key attached and held it up triumphantly.

Grandpa left the living room and came back with a large package. "Here it is, Fribble, with our wishes for a happy birthday." He set it down on the floor right in front of the big stuffed couch where the grown-ups could sit and watch. Grandma held Scamper on her lap.

Fribble knelt by his present and tore off the wrappings lickety-split. His heart beat fast as he stared at a beautiful wooden chest.

"It *is* a pirate's chest," Scamper shouted. "Told you," he crowed.

"I don't think it ever belonged to a pirate, Scamper," Grandma said. "But it *is* a chest for treasures. Grandpa and I thought you could put it at the foot of your bed, Fribble. It will make a good stool, and it's a place for your favorite things."

Fribble ran his paws over the ornate carving at the top of the chest. "It's a beauty," he said.

"When I saw it at an antique sale and noticed the initials 'F. M.' carved in the top, I knew it was meant for Fribble Mouse," she announced.

Fribble traced the two letters with his paw. Then he took his little silver key and opened the chest. Inside he found another package and opened it. "A White Paws baseball cap," he shouted. "Hurray! Thanks, Grandma and Grandpa," and he ran to give each of them a hug. Then he hurried back to his treasure chest.

Fribble saw that it was lined in red velvet, and he noticed a little red ribbon in one corner of the bottom of the chest. He gave it a tug. To Fribble's surprise the bottom lifted out. "Look," he said. "There's a secret compartment underneath."

"Well, I'll be," Grandpa said. "I never noticed that. Did you notice that?" he asked Grandma. She shook her head.

The space beneath was about two inches deep. Resting there were two envelopes. Fribble opened one and saw loose stamps inside. In another was a faded yellow newspaper clipping from the *Muenster Messenger* headed "Recent Happenings Around Town." Fribble handed it to Grandpa, and he read it out loud.

There was a birth announcement of a baby named Scurry Engels, a discussion of a party given by Dizzy and Mabel Wasley for visiting relatives, and a final item, saying that the local postmaster, Fleet Milton and his wife, Muffin, had returned to Muenster after an unforgettable adventure to Nashville, Tennessee.

"What was their unforgettable adventure, I wonder?" Fribble asked.

"Something special that they wouldn't ever forget," Grandpa said. "But who knows what it was? This paper is very old. It's dated June 5, 1877."

Fribble gathered the things back together, replaced the velvet bottom of the box, and locked it with his key. He put his key chain around his neck again, grabbed his White Paws hat, and said, "Come on, Grandpa. We have time to play catch with my new ball and glove before dinner."

Fribble and Scamper played catch with Grandpa, while the others visited inside. After the birthday feast, with all of Fribble's favorite foods including chocolate cheesecake, Fribble's father set the camera with a timer, so the whole family could crowd together for a happy family portrait.

That night, Fribble was sleepy on the drive home. He was ready to jump into bed as soon as he got home, but first, Fribble proudly set his treasure chest at the foot of his bed. He put his baseball cards, new ball, mitt, and cap inside, and then locked it.

On Sunday, Fribble lolled on the floor of his room and reexamined his treasure chest. He took out the false bottom again. Slowly he reread the clipping. Why had it been saved in the chest? Had one of the people named in the clipping owned the chest? Which one?

Suddenly Fribble sat bolt upright. *Of course.* Why hadn't he noticed right away? Fleet Milton. His initials were F. M. This treasure chest once belonged to the postmaster. The one who had an unforgettable adventure in Nashville in 1877. Where was Nashville, anyway? And what happened there that the post-master wouldn't forget? Fribble promised himself he'd find out on his next library visit.

On Tuesday, during library period at school, Miss Longwhiskers read a story to the class. Then she let the children spend the last part of their library period browsing and checking out books. Fribble went straight to the atlas. He had used it once before, but he wasn't sure he remembered how.

"May I help you with something, Fribble?" Miss Longwhiskers asked.

"I want to find out where Nashville is," Fribble said.

Miss Longwhiskers helped him find Nashville in the index. "But there are ten places called Nashville," Fribble said, running his paw down the page. "Which one do I want?"

"I don't know," Miss Longwhiskers said. "Which state are you looking for?"

Fribble shut his eyes tight and thought back to the newspaper clipping. Suddenly he remembered. "Nashville, Tennessee," he said.

Miss Longwhiskers helped him find it on the map of the United States.

Fribble sat for a long time looking at the map. Why had Fleet Milton gone all the way to Tennessee? Had he taken Fribble's treasure chest with him?

When Fribble got home from school on Tuesday, he dropped his backpack in his room, and then went downstairs to the kitchen for a snack. His mother had a big glass of milk and some cheese and crackers and slices of apple ready for him. Scamper, who never missed a chance to nibble, joined him.

"Want to play catch?" Scamper asked after he finished eating.

"No, I think I'll go to the library," Fribble announced, brushing cracker crumbs from his whiskers.

"Schoolwork?" asked his mother. "Are you working on a report?"

"No," Fribble said. "It's my treasure chest. I keep wondering about the postmaster who owned it and about his trip to Nashville. I want to find out all about him."

"It's all right to go," his mother said. "But don't be too long. I want you home before five o'clock so you can get your homework done before dinner."

"Can I come with you?" Scamper asked.

"Sure," Fribble said. "We'll be home by five," he promised his mother.

As they walked down the street toward the library, Scamper asked, "What kind of book are we looking for this time, Fribble?"

Fribble furrowed his brow. "I wish I knew," he said. "I want to find out more about the man who was the postmaster in Muenster back in 1877. But I don't know where to even start looking."

"Maybe there's a book about mailmen," Scamper suggested.

"I guess that's as good a place as any to start," Fribble agreed as they climbed the steps to the library.

Fribble went over to the computer catalog. First he clicked on the box that was marked "search the catalog." Then he clicked on "word." And finally, he typed in "mailman" and waited to see what book titles would appear. Scamper pulled a chair up beside his brother and knelt on it so that he could see the computer screen, too. Fourteen book titles came up on the screen. Fribble's nose twitched.

"Look at all these books," he said, smiling at Scamper.

But after he began to read the titles of the books, his smile disappeared. *"The Meddlesome Mailman, The Barefoot Mailman, What the Mailman Brought,"* he read aloud. "These are all fiction stories," Fribble said. "They won't tell us about Fleet Milton, the postmaster at Muenster. He was a real person."

Fribble stared at the screen again. "I think we're on the wrong track," he said.

"Let's ask Miss Scurry for help," suggested Scamper.

They walked over to Miss Scurry and told her their problem. She came back with them to the computer. "Instead of 'mailman,' let's try 'postal service,'" she suggested, and typed in the words. A number of interesting titles came up.

Miss Scurry, Fribble, and Scamper, all leaned in toward the computer screen, reading. "Here's a book that may help," Miss Scurry said, and pointed to one of the entries. Fribble noticed the excitement in her voice as she continued, "It's a list of post

offices and postmasters in the state from 1859 to 1959. The postmaster you're looking for should be one of the early ones listed."

Fribble felt his heart beating fast. There was a book about his postmaster or at least a book that would tell about Fleet Milton and lots of other postmasters.

Miss Scurry left them to hurry back to her desk and help another patron.

"Hurray, Fribble," Scamper said. "There is a mailman book. Now, let's go find it and check it out." He slid off his seat and started to leave. But then he came right back. "What number is it?" Scamper remembered that for a nonfiction book, you needed a call number to find it on the shelf.

Fribble wrote down the number, 383.49788 REFERENCE, on a slip of paper. For good measure, he added the author's name, William R. Baum.

Fribble and Scamper went over to the stacks of books. Quickly they found their way into the 300s. But they could not find the exact number they were looking for.

Again Fribble and Scamper went in search of Miss Scurry. Fribble showed her the slip of paper. "I know I wrote it down right," he said. "But I can't find the book."

"Oh," Miss Scurry said. "Yes, you have the right Dewey Decimal number, but see this word 'reference'? That means that this is a special book and it's kept in a special place. It can only be used in the library. People can't check it out."

"You mean we can't take it home and read it?" asked Scamper.

Scamper sounded mad, and Fribble didn't blame him. He was mad, too. After all, what was the point of having a book in the library if you couldn't check it out and read it?

"No, you can't take it home, but I'll help you find it and you can read it right here in the library," she explained. "This isn't a story to read. It's a book filled with information. You can look something up, and then I'll put it back on the shelf so that it's always ready for someone to use."

As she spoke, Miss Scurry led Fribble and Scamper to a special reference shelf. She lifted down the book and helped them find the Muenster Post Office and the date 1877. "Here you are," she said.

Fribble read aloud to Scamper, "Postmaster Fleet Milton, served from 1870 to 1891. Member of WFSC and APS." Fribble paused. That was all it said.

"What's that mean?" Scamper asked.

Fribble furrowed his brow. "I don't know," he said.

"I don't know, either," said Miss Scurry. "Maybe if you do more research, you'll find out. But I see I have two people waiting at my desk." She hurried off.

Fribble carefully copied the letters down into a little spiral notebook that he kept in his pocket. His long tail zigzagged through the air as it always did when he was excited. "I'll bet this is important, or they wouldn't list it in the book. Fleet Milton was a member of WFSC and APS a long, long time ago. They must be really old clubs."

"Aunty Q clubs?" asked Scamper.

"An-teek," Fribble said, correcting his brother. "I don't know if clubs can be antiques or not."

Fribble took the reference book back to Miss Scurry who was busy helping another woman, and he and Scamper left the library. As they walked home, Fribble said, "Why don't we stop and tell Miss Slippers what my silver key opened? We can stop at the antique shop and still get home in plenty of time for supper," he said.

"We're not supposed to go in there alone," Scamper said, shaking his head.

"We won't go inside the store," Fribble said.

Quickly they walked to the corner, then, with Fribble looking both ways, they crossed the street and hurried to Edam Street. In a few minutes they were standing just outside the antique shop.

Fribble looked at the little white cottage knowing that right inside was the baseball of his dreams, the home run ball signed by Slugger McGraw. He sighed, knowing that he could never afford such an expensive ball. Then he reminded himself, he wasn't here to look at a beautiful ball, he was here to tell Miss Slippers all about his treasure chest with its secret compartment. She would be excited to learn what his silver key had opened.

Fribble took his little brother's hand and led him up the walk to the door. He twisted the brass bell and listened to the loud "Brrrrrring" inside.

Miss Slippers opened the door. "Why, Scamper and Fribble! How nice to see you again." She stepped back. "Come in."

"We can't, Aunty Q," Scamper said. He rocked back and forth on his hind feet as he talked. "We're not supposed to go inside your antique shop without Mother 'cause you have so many breakable things."

Fribble said, "But we don't need to come in, Miss Slippers. You see, we're not really shopping today, but I wanted to tell you what my silver key opened."

"Oh, good," said Miss Slippers, "I want to hear all about it." She was wearing a light blue shawl over her pale gray dress, and she drew it tighter around her. Fribble noticed that today she was wearing gray slippers with blue satin ribbons. "But you know, it's a bit chilly out here," she said. "And even though you're not supposed to go inside antique shops alone, I think it would be all right if you visited me in my warm little kitchen. Why don't you follow those stepping stones, and I'll meet you at the back door."

Fribble and Scamper followed the path around to the back where Miss Slippers let them into her cheery kitchen. "Sit down," she suggested, pointing to two chairs at the round kitchen table. "I've just made some chamomile tea. That will warm us up while you tell me all about your antique key and what it opened."

"A tea party! Hurray!" Scamper said, as he quickly climbed into a chair.

Miss Slippers poured tea into three little cups, and fetched sugar and teaspoons. Fribble took a lump of sugar with a little tongs and watched as Scamper took three.

"Now," Miss Slippers said, leaning back to sip her tea. "Tell me all about your birthday present. What did that silver key of yours open?"

"It opened an antique chest," Fribble said. He fingered the silver key that dangled from the chain around his neck. "And inside was an 1877 newspaper clipping. After reading it, I figured out that the chest used to belong to Fleet Milton who was the postmaster of Muenster. Now I'm trying to learn more about him."

"We looked him up in a book," Scamper added, between sips.

"The book gave us a clue. It said Fleet Milton was a member of APS and WFSC," Fribble said, after pulling out and looking in his little notebook. "Whatever those clubs are that he was a member of, they're more than a hundred years old. That makes them antiques, right? Do you know what those initials mean?"

Without giving her a chance to answer, Scamper said, "Since it's a treasure chest, do you think maybe the 'P' in APS stands for pirate?" As he asked, Scamper dropped a fourth lump of sugar into his tiny teacup and stirred.

Fribble sighed. "How many times do I have to tell you, Scamper? Fleet Milton wasn't a pirate. He was a postmaster."

Paying no attention to his brother, Scamper added, "And do you think maybe the 'C' in WFSC stands for cheese?"

Miss Slippers smiled and took another sip of tea. "I really don't think that APS stands for the American Pirate's Society. And I don't think WFSC stands for the World Federation for Sharp Cheese."

"Well, what *do* you think those letters stand for?" Fribble asked.

"My guess is they have something to do with the post office."

Fribble thoughtfully stroked his whiskers. "Maybe I should ask the postmaster of Cheddarville."

"I think you're right!" Miss Slippers said.

"Who *is* the postmaster of Cheddarville?" asked Scamper.

"His name is Mr. Bernie Bramble," said Miss Slippers.

"Could we phone him at work?" Fribble asked.

"It's just about closing time at the post office," Miss Slippers said, glancing at a little clock that sat on her shelf.

Fribble followed her glance and said, "Yikes! It's almost five o'clock." He quickly slid out of the kitchen chair. "We have to hurry home. Thanks, Miss Slippers. You've been a big help."

"And thanks for the tea, Aunty Q," added Scamper. "It was good."

"I'm glad you came by," Miss Slippers said. "Come again, and let me know what you learn, won't you?"

Fribble took Scamper by the paw and quickly led the way across the stepping stones, out the front gate, and down the street. He didn't slow down or let go of his little brother's paw until they were on their own front porch. "We're home," he called to his mother in the kitchen as they entered the house. "And I'm going up to my room to do my homework."

Fribble was glad that his homework was math. Math was easy for him, and he finished his problems quickly.

Over dinner, Fribble talked about the mysterious initials, APS and WFSC. What could they stand for? After the table was cleared, Fribble said to his mother, "Is it all right if I call the postmaster at home and ask him about the initials?"

"I suppose so," his mother said. "But remember Mr. Bramble is a busy man, so don't waste his time. And be sure to thank him for his help."

"All right," Fribble said. He looked up Bernie Bramble in the telephone book and dialed the number. Scamper hovered near the phone. When Mr. Bramble answered, Fribble explained about the antique birthday chest that might have belonged to the postmaster of Muenster. He said, "I looked him up in a post office book that said he was a member of APS and WFSC. Since he was a postmaster and you're a postmaster, I thought you might know what those initials stand for."

"I certainly do," said Mr. Bramble. "APS stands for the American Philatelic Society. And WFSC stands for Wisconsin Federation of Stamp Collectors. Both groups are for people who have an interest in stamp collecting."

"Wow!" said Fribble. His nose twitched and his tail lashed through the air. "Mr. Bramble, how do you spell that word, 'phil-a-whatever'?"

Fribble carefully wrote out the word "philatelic" letter by letter as Mr. Bramble spelled it to him.

"Thanks so much for your help," Fribble said before he hung up.

"Does the 'P' stand for pirate?" Scamper asked.

"No," Fribble explained, "Not pirate. Philatelic. It has to do with stamps."

That night, Fribble fell asleep thinking about stamps. He dreamed of stamps, and they were the first things he thought of the next morning. After Fribble walked his brother to school and left him at the kindergarten playground, he went inside to the library to the computer catalog. Miss Longwhiskers came over and asked if she could be of help.

"I want to read about stamps and stamp collecting clubs," Fribble explained.

While she watched, Fribble typed 'stamp collecting' into the computer catalog. Several titles came up. Fribble decided on *Beginning Stamp Collecting*. Its number was 769.56075. Off he went to the 700s. Miss Longwhiskers helped him locate the book.

"Hey!" Fribble said. "Here's another good one." He picked up another book called *Getting Started in Stamp Collecting*.

"That's one of the good things about the numbers we put on these books," Miss Longwhiskers explained. "It's called the Dewey Decimal system. Books written about the same subject have similar numbers and are placed on the same shelf."

Fribble checked out both books. He was eager to sit and read them, but the bell rang and he had to head for class. He promised himself he'd read them tonight as soon as he got home. He'd learn more about Fleet Milton's hobby. But would that help him find out why the postmaster had gone to Nashville? And why his trip was an unforgettable adventure?

Fribble dashed home from school, scarfed down his snack, and without being asked, went upstairs to do his homework. Fortunately, he didn't have much.

When it was done, he breathed a satisfied sigh. Finally he had time to read and learn a little more about the hobby of his favorite postmaster, Fleet Milton. Fribble's nose gave a little twitch of joyful expectation.

Fribble lay on his stomach on his bed and happily started thumbing through the two books about stamp collecting that he'd checked out from the school library. In no time at all, Fribble was hooked on stamps. Wouldn't it be fun to start a stamp collection? No wonder postmaster Fleet Milton was a collector.

As he lay there, looking at one fascinating stamp after another, Fribble felt a little nagging memory at the back of his mind. Had he forgotten something? Something important? What was it? He sat up straight and thought hard. He knew he was right on the edge of remembering what it was. Yes! He already owned some stamps! The loose stamps in the envelope in his treasure chest!

Quickly Fribble jumped up and went to kneel beside his treasure chest at the foot of his bed. He unlocked it and pulled out his baseball cards, mitt, cap, and ball, and dumped them in a heap on the floor. When the chest was empty, he pulled the little velvet tab and removed the bottom, revealing the secret compartment underneath.

Fribble remembered that there were two envelopes in the secret compartment of his birthday chest. One held the old newspaper clipping, and the other had stamps in it. Fribble took out the envelopes and found the one that held two loose stamps. The stamps seemed to be identical. Fribble took them over to the window where he could get the best light to examine them.

They were pale blue. At the bottom of the stamp were the words, "five cents." On the right and the left was the numeral "5" in a small circle. In the center of the stamp was a drawing of a big hot air balloon with the name "Buffalo" written on it. And at the top, it said "Balloon Postage."

Fribble frowned and sat very still, slowly stroking his whiskers. Balloon Postage? What could that mean? He knew that letters got to his house in a mail truck. And he knew that some letters, marked "airmail," were flown across the country in planes. But he didn't know of any mail that ever went by balloon.

Fribble carefully put the stamps and the newspaper clipping away, replaced the red velvet bottom, and put his baseball stuff back into the chest. Then he leaped up, checked to see that he had his little spiral notebook and a stubby pencil in his pocket, grabbed his jacket, and raced down the stairs.

In the kitchen, Fribble stopped to tell his mother he was off to the public library.

"Again?" his mother said. "What are you looking for now?"

"More information about stamps," Fribble explained.

"Can I come, too?" Scamper called from the family room where he had been building a castle with his blocks.

"Sure," Fribble agreed, "but hurry up."

They walked quickly down the street to the library. Miss Scurry smiled when she saw them. "What are you two looking for this time?" she asked.

"Balloons," Fribble said. "I think I know how to find them." He led Scamper right past the librarian's desk and over to a computer. Fribble clicked on "search the catalog," then on "word," and finally entered, "balloon."

To his astonishment, the computer screen said there were 93 titles that matched his search. Fribble quickly started to read and dismiss them, one after another: *Making Balloon Animals*, *Taking a Balloon Ride*, *Belinda's Balloon*, *Benjamin's Balloon*, *The Silver Balloon*, *The Red Balloon*. "Drat," Fribble said. "None of these are what I want. I guess typing in 'balloon' isn't enough. I'll try 'airmail balloon.'"

Carefully Fribble typed in the words. This time there was only one match. Fribble read the description. This book was a fiction story about a little girl who wanted to send someone by balloon to the moon. He groaned.

"This book won't help, either," Fribble said. His whiskers drooped.

"What kind of book are you trying to find?" Scamper asked.

"I'm trying to find a book that will tell me if the mail was ever sent by balloon," Fribble said.

"Maybe we need help from Miss Scurry," Scamper suggested.

Fribble went to the librarian and told her what he was looking for.

She looked puzzled. "That's a hard question," she said, leading the way back to the computerized catalog. "Let's try 'airmail history' and see if that gives us anything."

Up came a title on the computer screen, *Flying the Mail*. Its call number was 383.14409. "Why don't we take a look? Maybe it will mention balloons," Miss Scurry said. Fribble wrote down the call number, and all three of them went to search.

Fribble found the book and carried it to a table. He stared at the heavy book filled with small print. "I don't think this book is for second graders," he said. "It'll take forever to read."

"It's for adults," Miss Scurry agreed. "But you don't have to read it all. Let me show you. We'll look up 'balloon' in the index and see if it's mentioned." She flipped to the back of the book and ran her finger down the index, until she saw "balloon." "It's here!" Her voice sounded excited.

Fribble leaned in close to see where she was pointing. "Thanks," he said, pulling the book closer to him. "It says to look on page 127." Quickly he thumbed through the pages. On page 127, he saw the heading 'Balloons' and he began to read aloud. "Balloons have sometimes been used to carry letters. They carried mail during the Franco-Prussian War, and in 1877, in the United States, balloons were used to deliver mail with the first airmail stamp during a flight by an American balloonist, Samuel Archer King." Fribble stopped reading. "In 1877?" he said. "Wow! That's the same year as the news-paper clipping about postmaster Fleet Milton."

"What else does the book say?" asked Scamper.

"Nothing," Fribble said. His whiskers drooped again. "That's all."

"It was pretty short," Miss Scurry agreed, "but it did give us two valuable clues about where to look next."

"What clues?" Fribble asked.

"Well, it mentioned the first airmail stamp."

"Is there a book of firsts?" Fribble asked.

"As a matter of fact, there is," Miss Scurry said. "On our reference shelf we have a book called *Famous First Facts.*" She led the way to the reference section, took down the book, and handed it to Fribble.

"Do we look in the index?" Fribble asked as he carried the book to a table.

"That's right," Miss Scurry said.

"Under 'balloon' or what?" asked Scamper.

"Try 'postal service,'" suggested Miss Scurry.

She watched as Fribble turned to the back of the book to find the index and then looked down the entries.

"It's here!" Fribble squeaked. "There's lots of things under 'postal service.'"

"Look for 'stamps,' and then 'balloon,'" said Miss Scurry.

Fribble looked down the list.

"What's it say?" asked Scamper.

"We need to look at page 216."

Fribble turned to that page and found a short entry. He read it aloud. "The world's first adhesive airmail stamp was issued in 1877 for a private flight by American balloonist Samuel Archer King. Only 300 stamps were printed. The stamp was used on mail carried from Nashville on June 1, 1877. The wind carried the Buffalo Balloon to Gallatin, Tennessee, 26 miles from its starting point."

"Nashville!" Fribble's eyes shone. "Remember postmaster Fleet Milton went there. And just think!" Fribble said. "They only made 300 Buffalo Balloon stamps, and I've got two of them!"

Deep in thought, Fribble slowly turned to the librarian. "You said we had two clues. One clue was that the Buffalo Balloon was the first airmail stamp. What's the other clue?"

Miss Scurry smiled. "The book also gave us the name of the balloonist who flew the first adhesive airmail stamp. It was Samuel Archer King. Remember?"

"Right!" Fribble said, and his long tail lashed through the air. "Would there be a book about him in biographies?"

"That's a good idea, Fribble, though I don't think our library has a whole book about him," she said. "But it's worth checking the computer catalog."

Miss Scurry and Scamper followed along as Fribble quickly went to a computer and typed in the name "Samuel Archer King." There were no matches. Fribble sat back in the seat and sighed. He wished he could read more about first balloon mail flight. Lots of folks must have watched it. Maybe postmaster Fleet Milton was there. Where else could he look?

Suddenly Fribble squeaked and sat up straight. Of course. "The Internet," he said out loud.

"Another good idea," Miss Scurry agreed, "and you know how to use it. Let me know if you need help or if you find anything." Off she went back to her desk to assist a woman who was waiting.

Fribble slid out of his seat and headed to one of the library computers that was connected with the Internet. Scamper followed closely on his heels. Fribble typed in Samuel Archer King's name. Several sites popped up. Fribble clicked on the first one and began to read, mumbling to himself.

"What does it say?" Scamper demanded.

"Lots of stuff," Fribble said. "King made dozens of balloon trips. And they didn't all turn out well. His balloon was called the Buffalo, and it drifted wherever it wanted to go. Sometimes he landed in the trees."

"Ouch!" Scamper said. "Did Mr. King fly all by himself? Did he go very far?"

"It says here that a big crowd of people saw him off the day he took the airmail. He went 26 miles from Nashville, Tennessee, to Gallatin, Tennessee, and he tossed some of the letters overboard as he went."

"He threw the letters away?" Scamper said. "Boy, I wouldn't want him for a mailman."

"Well," Fribble said, "it says that he hoped people who found them would take the letters to a post office. And the letters he didn't toss overboard, he mailed himself at the post office in Gallatin."

Fribble looked at another entry. "This one is called, 'Postmasters gather for the big balloon event.'" Quickly Fribble clicked on this site and began to read the article that came up. It was an old newspaper story from the *Nashville Gazette* dated June 1, 1877.

"What's it say?" asked Scamper.

"It's written by a reporter called John Lillard. It says J. H. Snively designed the Buffalo Balloon stamp and that only 23 were used. And listen to this!" Fribble's whiskers were aquiver. "Postmasters from all over came to the big event including Amos Brooke from Swisslund, Illinois; Nibbles Trapp from Brieton, Missouri; and Fleet Milton from Muenster, Wisconsin."

Fribble jumped to his feet in excitement as he read this last bit of news. "Our very own postmaster, Fleet Milton, was there watching the Buffalo Balloon take off!" Fribble said. His eyes glittered with excitement. "I'll bet he bought the stamps that day and saved them in his special box."

"Let's tell Miss Scurry what you found," Scamper said.

With great excitement, Fribble and Scamper went over to the librarian's desk. "Guess what?" Fribble said. "The postmaster from Muenster *was* at the first airmail balloon trip. It says so in an old newspaper article on the Internet."

Miss Scurry went with them back to the computer. After she read the article, she seemed almost as excited as they were. She printed out a copy of the newspaper article and gave it to Fribble.

"You know, Fribble," Miss Scurry said. "I'm not a stamp collector, and your Buffalo Balloon isn't an official stamp printed by the U.S. government, but it

does seem to be a rather special stamp. Sometimes old stamps are worth a lot of money."

"Really?" Fribble said. "But it says right on my stamp that it's only worth five cents."

"The stamp may have been worth five cents in postage back in 1877, but that was a very long time ago. More than a hundred years."

"It's an antique," said Fribble.

"I don't think they usually call stamps antiques," Miss Scurry said. "But they are called 'collectibles.' There are books on collecting stamps and coins. I know their value depends on how rare they are and what condition they are in. In some special shops you can buy stamps and coins. Someone in one of those shops could probably tell you just how much your stamp is worth."

Fribble and Scamper said goodbye to Miss Scurry and headed for home. Fribble had a lot on his mind. Were the stamps in his special baseball chest really valuable? If they were, did he want to sell them? He thought of the autographed baseball in Miss Slippers's antique shop that he'd love to buy if he only had enough money. Should he sell the stamps and buy the ball, or save them and start his own collection? It would be exciting to collect stamps just like postmaster Fleet Milton. And he could start his collection with a Buffalo Balloon stamp.

Fribble didn't know what he wanted to do. He was confused and needed to talk with someone. "Let's stop and visit Miss Slippers," he suggested. "She'll want to know what we found out."

"Aunty Q?" asked Scamper. A happy smile spread over his face. "Do you think she'll make us tea?"

"Maybe," Fribble said.

They turned down the block to Edam Street and Fribble was soon twisting the old bell on Miss Slippers's shop. When she came to the door and found Fribble and Scamper, Miss Slippers smiled. "Hello. What a good time for you to stop by. I was just thinking of making myself a cup of tea. Would you two join me?"

"Yes!" Scamper quickly said.

"All right then, I'll meet you at the back kitchen door."

Once inside, it took no time at all for Miss Slippers to brew a pot of chamomile tea and set cups and saucers on the table, along with a plate of cookies.

As they sipped and nibbled, Fribble told Miss Slippers about their recent discoveries at the library.

"My, my," she said. "You've been busy."

"But I can't decide what to do," Fribble said. "If the stamps are really valuable like Miss Scurry thinks, I could sell them and maybe buy Slugger McGraw's autographed home run ball. But I've been reading about stamps, and I think I might want to start my own collection. The Buffalo Balloon would be a great one to start with."

"That is a hard choice," Miss Slippers agreed. "And only you can decide. Take your time. Those stamps have been waiting in the postmaster's chest for well over a hundred years. They can wait a few more days until you're sure you know what you want to do."

After their tea, Fribble and Scamper thanked Miss Slippers and started for home. While they walked along, Scamper chatted about how much he liked tea and cookies at Aunty Q's, but Fribble was quiet and thoughtful. He was still busy thinking. What should he do about his stamps?

Over dinner, Fribble said, "I used the yellow pages of the phone book to look up stamp shops in town. There's one on Bridge Street. I was wondering if maybe I could go there on Saturday and ask someone in the shop about my stamps?"

"I think that's a smart idea," Fribble's father said. "I'd be glad to drive you there."

"Thanks, Dad," Fribble said.

"Can I come, too?" asked Scamper.

"Of course," his father agreed. "It might be a good idea, Fribble, to call ahead of time and make sure that the owner or someone who knows a lot about stamps will be there on Saturday morning. You'll need to talk to someone who can answer your questions."

"I'll call the shop tomorrow right after school," Fribble promised.

That night, before he went to bed, Fribble took the key from around his neck and opened his box. He pulled out his baseball stuff and then removed the bottom of the box and took out the envelope with the stamps in it. Fribble took the stamps over to the bedside lamp and studied them closely. He wanted to be the proud owner of the Slugger McGraw home run baseball, and if he sold the stamps, he might have enough money to buy it. But he liked owning the Buffalo Balloon stamps, too. Fribble felt pulled in two directions.

Right after school on Thursday, Fribble ate his snack at home and then got down the telephone book. He looked in the yellow pages under Stamps—Collectors and found the Bridge Street Stamp and Coin Shop. He dialed the number.

"Bridge Street Stamp and Coin Shop. Dusty Squint speaking. May I help you?" asked a friendly sounding man.

"I hope so," Fribble said. "I have two old stamps, and I'd like to bring them in to show you and find out how much they're worth."

"I see," said the voice. "And when did you want to come in?"

"My father can bring me Saturday morning."

"I'll be here," said the man. "I'm the owner of the shop, and I'll be glad to try to help you."

"Do you buy stamps?" asked Fribble.

"Yes, I buy and sell them," said Mr. Squint. "What's your name?"

"My name is Fribble."

"Well, Fribble, I'll look forward to seeing you and your stamps on Saturday."

Fribble hung up the phone. In just two days, an expert would be looking at his stamps. Fribble quivered in anticipation.

On Friday morning, Fribble walked Scamper to school and left him at the playground. Then Fribble went in the library to see Miss Longwhiskers.

"Hello, Fribble," she said when she saw him come in. "What can I help you find today?"

"I was wondering if our library has any books about stamp collecting?" Fribble asked. "I read two from the downtown library, and I'd like to read more."

"Why, I didn't know you were interested in stamps, Fribble."

"I am," Fribble said, "but I don't know much about them yet."

"If you decide to become a stamp collector, you'll have a lot of company," Miss Longwhiskers said. "One out of every ten people in the United States collects stamps. In fact, I'm a stamp collector myself."

"Really?" Fribble said.

"Yes, and we have a good book on stamp collecting as a hobby." Miss Longwhiskers didn't even have to look it up. She led Fribble straight to the 700s in the nonfiction section. "Did you see the article in the newspaper last weekend about the new stamp that's coming out?" she asked, as she helped Fribble find a book called *Your Hobby: Stamp Collecting.*

Fribble happily clutched the book in has paws. "No, I didn't see anything about stamps in the paper," he said.

"Let me show you." Miss Longwhiskers led Fribble to the spot where they kept the newspapers. She picked up the *Cheddarville Times* from last Sunday and began to thumb through it. "Here it is," she said, handing the paper to him.

Fribble spread the newspaper out on the table and began to read. The article said that the government was printing a stamp to honor the one hundredth anniversary of Orville and Wilbur Wright's first flight. It would be a 37-cent stamp.

"Wow!" Fribble said. "It says here that they are printing 85 million of these stamps! I want one. Will it only cost 37 cents?"

"Yes," Miss Longwhiskers said. "The first day they're out, only two post offices will sell them. But the very next day, you'll be able to buy them at any post office."

"Even here in Cheddarville?" asked Fribble.

"Yes, indeed."

Fribble checked out the stamp collecting book and sat down to read it until the bell rang. He was fascinated to learn about an island in the South Pacific that sent its mail by tin can. No planes came to the little island, and coral reefs prevented big ships from reaching it. So swimmers pushed the mail out to boats in five-gallon tin cans. Once, when Fribble turned a page in the book, his heart skipped a beat. There was a picture of a hot air balloon stamp! But it wasn't the Buffalo Balloon. It was a balloon called Jupiter.

When the bell rang, Fribble reluctantly closed his book and went to class. He'd read more later, he promised himself. After all, he thought, there's no reason why a baseball player can't also be a stamp collector. That night he had trouble falling asleep. He kept wondering what he'd learn at the stamp shop the next day.

When it was almost time to leave for the Bridge Street Stamp and Coin Shop on Saturday morning, Fribble was jumping up and down in excitement. At five minutes to ten, Fribble ran to his treasure chest, closely followed by Scamper, unlocked it with the key, dumped all his baseball stuff out of it, and then removed the bottom. He took out the envelope holding the two stamps.

Instead of shoving the envelope into his pocket where it might get crushed, Fribble carried it carefully in his paws. He knew now that condition was important, and he didn't want to add a crease or wrinkle to the stamps.

On the drive to the shop, Fribble held the envelope in his lap in one paw and nervously smoothed his whiskers with the other.

There was a parking place right in front, and they had to walk only a few steps to the shop. Once inside, Fribble hurried straight to the counter where they were greeted by a roly-poly mouse with a smile on his face.

"Mr. Squint?" Fribble tightly clutched his envelope of stamps.

"That's me, and you must be Fribble."

"Yes, I'm Fribble, and this is my father and my brother," Fribble answered.

"Glad to see all of you. I'm Dusty Squint," he said. "What kind of stamps do you have?"

"They're both Buffalo Balloon stamps," Fribble said.

"Really? And what do they look like?"

"Blue with a balloon in the center, and it says five cents across the bottom."

"If they're real Buffalo Balloon stamps, and they're in good condition, they could be worth quite a bit of money," Mr. Squint said. "Let's have a peek."

Fribble placed the envelope on the counter. Dusty reached in, using a pair of tongs to withdraw the stamps from the envelope. "You need to be very careful with valuable stamps," he explained. He laid the stamps on a velvet pad and carefully examined them with a magnifying glass.

Fribble shot a look at his father and his brother. Were they as nervous as he was? Then he turned toward Mr. Squint, watched, waited, and held his breath.

Mr. Squint took his time with each stamp, looking at the front and back. Fribble's nose quivered and his tail whipped through the air. Just when Fribble thought he might burst with excitement or fall over in a faint, Mr. Squint smiled.

"You're right," he said, looking at Fribble. "You have two genuine balloon stamps in good condition."

Fribble exhaled. He felt so relieved his legs were wobbly.

"How do you come to have these?" Mr. Squint asked.

Fribble explained about the antique birthday chest and how he learned that postmaster Fleet Milton had gone to Nashville, Tennessee, in 1877 to watch Samuel Archer King fly in the Buffalo Balloon.

"You have two great stamps," Mr. Squint said.

"Are they worth lots and lots of money?" asked Scamper.

Fribble was embarrassed that his little brother blurted out this question, but truthfully, that was exactly what he wanted to know, too.

Mr. Squint pulled out a book. It was a Scott Specialized Catalog. He used the index and then quickly flipped to a page. It took him only a moment to locate the Buffalo Balloon stamp. "Here it is," he said. "This is what you would pay if you went in a store to buy each of these stamps."

He pushed the book toward them and pointed to a price next to a picture of the stamp. The price was a two, followed by a lot of zeros. "Two hundred dollars?" Fribble said. His eyes opened wide.

"No," Mr. Squint corrected him. "Two thousand dollars. Of course a dealer, like me, doesn't pay that much. We buy stamps, for a lot less money than they're worth, because we have to run our shops and pay the people who work here, and sometimes we have to keep stamps for a long time before a customer comes in who wants them."

"How much would you pay for one of my stamps?" asked Fribble.

"I could give you $1,500 for each of them," said Mr. Squint.

Fribble's father looked shocked. "I'm amazed," he said.

"Well, the Buffalo Balloon is an old and valuable stamp," Mr. Squint said.

"Wow!" Fribble said. "So much money! Is it really up to me, Dad?"

"Yes, son," his father said. "That chest was your birthday present, so you get to decide what you want to do."

Fribble made up his mind quickly. "I'll sell you one of them," he said. "But I want to keep the other one to start my own collection."

"Going to be a collector, are you?" asked Mr. Squint. "That's great. I'll toss in a stamp album for free. You may become a good customer."

Only a few minutes later, Fribble, his father, and Scamper left the Bridge Street Stamp and Coin Shop. Fribble carried a handsome new stamp album with his Buffalo Balloon stamp in it, and he carried a check made out to him for $1,500.

"Whatcha going to do with your money?" Scamper asked on the way home.

Fribble smiled. "I'm going to buy Slugger's baseball," he said, "And I have a plan for the rest."

Fribble was a good math student. And he did some quick calculating of how much money he had to spend as they drove home in the car.

He knew that he had more than enough to buy Slugger McGraw's baseball. Miss Slippers had said that it would cost $200. It made him very happy to think of owning that wonderful ball. Fribble wanted to make the rest of his family just as happy as he was over his good luck. Who would have guessed that his silver key would unlock such good fortune?

Fribble fingered the key around his neck as he thought about his plan.

"Dad," Fribble asked, "would you drop me off at Miss Slippers's Antique Shop on our way home?"

"Of course," his father said. "I thought you might want to go there."

"You're going to Aunty Q's? Can I go, too?" asked Scamper.

"Not this time," Fribble said. Then looking at his brother's sad face, he quickly added, "I'm not going to tea, Scamper. I have to talk business with Miss Slippers. But we'll go again soon to visit, I promise."

At the Antique Shop, Fribble hopped out and quickly shut the car door in order to avoid an argument from Scamper. As the car drove away, Fribble went up to the shop and rang the funny old bell. "Brrrrrring." He heard it sounding through the shop. In just a moment, Miss Slippers opened the door. Today she was wearing a blue dress with yellow roses on it and Fribble noticed that she was wearing blue slippers with yellow ribbons to match.

"Why, hello, Fribble," Miss Slippers said. And she looked about. "Where's Scamper today?"

"He's at home," Fribble explained, "because I'm here on business today."

"I see. Well then, come in."

Fribble walked over to the desk where Miss Slippers kept her cash register. He showed her his check from the Bridge Street Stamp and Coin Shop.

Miss Slippers gasped. "Oooh, Fribble! You must have sold your Buffalo Balloon stamps."

"Only one of them," Fribble explained. "It's a lot of money, isn't it?"

"Yes, indeed," Miss Slippers agreed.

"And I have a plan for it," Fribble went on. "I want to buy a present for everyone in my family. I know Scamper would like to have that little rocking chair he tried out the first day we came to your shop. Mother loved the china set with the tiny violets. And my father would be so proud to carry that hundred-year-old pocket watch that belonged to Colonel Beauregard Chapman. And of course, I want to buy Slugger McGraw's home run ball. Do I have enough money to do all that?"

"Good gracious, me. Let's see," said Miss Slippers. She took the spectacles that dangled on a ribbon around her neck and perched them on the end of her nose. Then she took a piece of paper and began writing down some numbers.

"The baseball is $200. The gold watch is $250. The rocking chair is $100. And that china set is

$350." She added up the numbers. "That comes to $900," she said.

"You certainly have enough, with some left over."

"Great!" Fribble said. "And I want to buy something for Grandma and Grandpa, too. After all, they gave me the treasure chest."

"What do you have in mind?" asked Miss Slippers.

"On my birthday, my dad took a family picture of us all. He had an enlargement made to give them when we go there on our next trip. I thought maybe I could get a fancy frame for that picture."

Miss Slippers led the way to the back of the shop where there were paintings and frames. "Here's a beautiful crystal frame that will hold an 8" x 10" photo," she said. "Do you like it?"

"Yes," Fribble said. "It glitters in the light. It's perfect! And I'll still have some money left over to put in my bank account."

Miss Slippers did more figuring. "You'll have $500 left to put in the bank," she said. "Now, do your parents know that you're doing this?" she asked.

"My father knows I'm here," Fribble said. "He drove me."

"Still, I think I'd better phone your home and make sure it's all right with them for you to be spending so much money," she said.

Fribble's whiskers drooped. "But I wanted it to be a surprise."

"Tell you what," she suggested. "I'll call and say that you want to buy something, but I won't mention what. Okay?"

"Sure," said Fribble, "just don't give away the surprise. Please."

As Miss Slippers called and talked with Fribble's father, Fribble stood nearby; his tail zipped back and forth through the air.

Finally Miss Slippers hung up and smiled at him. "Your father says that since the chest was your birthday gift and you solved the mystery yourself, the money is yours to spend any way you want."

Fribble let out a sigh of relief.

"We'll pack up all the things you want and I'll drive you home in my van," Miss Slippers offered. "You can surprise everyone at once that way. All right?"

"Yes!" Fribble agreed. He bounced up and down in excitement as he watched Miss Slippers pack everything up. The ball, chair, watch, and picture frame were easy. But it took a long time to pack the china dishes so they wouldn't break. Each piece was wrapped in soft tissue paper before going into a big box.

Fribble helped her carry everything to the van and store it in the back. Then they made the short trip to Fribble's house.

Miss Slippers suggested that they leave everything in the van for the moment.

Fribble brought her inside to Scamper's great joy and his parents' surprise.

"Aunty Q," Scamper said, running to give her a hug.

"Hello, Scamper," she said.

Then Miss Slippers told Fribble's parents she had some "surprises" out in the van.

Everyone trooped out to the van and helped carry things inside. Fribble giggled as he saw from their faces they'd figured out there were presents for everyone. Scamper immediately tore off the wrappings, sat in his little rocking chair, and beamed. He rocked back and forth with his eyes squeezed shut and a look of bliss on his face.

Fribble proudly puffed out his little chest as he handed a small package to his father. Then he gleefully watched the look of astonishment that came over his father's face as he held the gold watch in his paws. Fribble's mother sat at the dining table holding one delicate tea cup and saucer with a small tear in her eye.

Finally, Fribble's father put the family photograph in the frame.

"Grandma and Grandpa will love it," Fribble said, as everyone admired how great they all looked smiling out from the sparkling frame.

Miss Slippers left with an invitation to come to tea next Sunday when Fribble's mother planned to use her new dishes for the first time.

Fribble raced up the stairs to his room carrying the black marble stand and Slugger McGraw's home run ball. He cleared space on the top of a dresser and set the stand right next to his brand new stamp collecting book. Then he put the ball in place, being sure that the two signatures faced out to the room. Fribble sat quietly on his wooden chest, gazing at his treasures.

His dream had come true, and everyone else in Fribble's family was happy, too. It was all thanks to

Fleet Milton, the Muenster postmaster, who had hidden those Buffalo Balloon stamps in a secret place, locked safely away by the silver key.